OUT OF CONTROL,
Ms Wiz

D0034179

TERENCE BLACKER

OUT OF CONTROL, Ms Wiz

Illustrated by
TONY ROSS

ANDERSEN PRESS
LONDON

First published in Great Britain in 2009 by
ANDERSEN PRESS LIMITED
20 Vauxhall Bridge Road
London SW1V 2SA
www.andersenpress.co.uk

2 3 4 5 6 7 8 9 10

In Stitches with Ms Wiz first published in 1989 by Piccadilly Press Limited
In Control, Ms Wiz? first published in 1990 by Piccadilly Press Limited

British Library Cataloguing in Publication Data available.

ISBN 978 184 270 847 7

Printed and bound in Great Britain by Clays Ltd, Elcograf S.p.A.

IN STITCHES WITH
Ms Wiz

IN CONTROL,
Ms Wiz?

67

IN STITCHES WITH
Ms Wiz

For Xan

CHAPTER ONE
A PAIN ON THURSDAY

Have you ever seen an ambulance racing at top speed through the streets, overtaking cars, driving through red traffic lights, its siren blaring and its blue light flashing? Have you ever thought that it would be exciting to be riding in the back, behind the darkened windows of the ambulance?

Well, it isn't.

Jack Beddows loved going fast – he had always thought that he would like to be a fireman or policeman one day so that he could break the speed limit whenever he felt like it – but right now, as he lay in the back of an ambulance travelling at sixty miles an

hour down a busy street, he wasn't interested. In fact, he would have given anything to be back at home, lying in his bed, without this terrible pain in his stomach.

It was the worst stomach ache of all time and it had been getting more painful all day. It was so bad that he hadn't been able to concentrate at school. In the middle of the maths lesson, he had even started crying.

"Please, sir." Jack's friend Caroline had put up her hand. "Jack's feeling ill."

The new teacher, Mr Bailey, had continued writing on the blackboard. "I'm not surprised," he had said. "I felt ill when I looked at his work this morning."

"But sir—" Caroline had protested.

"Nice try, Jack," said Mr Bailey. "Just in time for the maths test on Monday. Very convenient, I must say."

The ambulance took a corner with a screech of tyres. Jack groaned.

If only Ms Wiz had still been at school, he thought. She had been the class teacher last term and, whenever there were problems, she somehow made it better with her magic spells. There was certainly nothing magic about Mr Bailey.

When Jack hobbled home after school, he had found his father messing around with the car, as usual.

"Dad," Jack had said to the pair of legs sticking out from under the car. "I've got a pain in my stomach."

His father continued working. "Have you been?" he asked eventually.

That was the sum total of his father's medical knowledge. Even when his little sister Jenny had complained of having toothache, it had been the same old question. Have you been?

By the time his mother had come back from the library where she worked, Jack had been sick twice.

"Down in the dumps?" she had asked cheerfully. "A bit under the weather?"

"No. Ill."

"Why not go and skateboard outside?"

"I'm too ill to skateboard."

"Ring the doctor, Dad," said Mrs Beddows. "I think it's serious."

It certainly felt serious, Jack thought as the ambulance finally came to a halt.

7

The doors swung open. Jack was put on a trolley and wheeled into the hospital.

The nurse in the main hall looked down at Jack. "How are we?" she asked.

Jack smiled weakly. "We're not very well," he said.

"Children's ward," said the nurse to the man pushing Jack's trolley. "The doctor will be right along. I'll get them to prepare the theatre."

Theatre? thought Jack as he was wheeled into a brightly-coloured ward. Here I am, dying, and they're talking about the theatre. Weird.

The other children in the ward stared as a nurse drew the curtains around Jack's bed.

"Just slip out of your clothes," she said, "and pop into this."

She gave Jack what looked like a nightie.

"I'm a boy," he protested feebly.

"And this is a gown," said the nurse. "Hurry up. The Consultant will be here in a minute."

Jack had just put on his gown when a tall man with a white coat poked his head around the curtains. The Consultant stood by Jack's bed and looked down at him like a vulture considering its breakfast. Behind him stood another doctor. She had her dark hair in a bun and wore rather peculiar glasses. Something about the way she smiled at him reminded Jack of someone he knew.

"Let's have a quick look at you," said the Consultant, pressing the right side of Jack's stomach with his cold hands.

"Ow," said Jack.

"Mm. Uncomfortable?"

"Yes," said Jack.

The Consultant turned to the nurse.

"Are the parents here?" he asked.

"They've been delayed," she said. "Apparently they were trying to follow the ambulance and had a small disagreement with a double-decker bus. They're all right. They rang to give their permission to operate."

Jack groaned. His first time in hospital and his father had driven into a bus while chasing the ambulance. Typical.

"We're going to give you a little operation," the Consultant said to Jack, as if it were some kind of treat. "We need to take out your appendix to make you feel better."

"What's an appendix?"

"It's a small, completely useless piece of gristle in your intestine," said the Consultant. "I promise you won't miss it. Now we'd better hurry because that naughty appendix really ought to come out soon."

That's just great, thought Jack, as he was wheeled off once again. I'm about to be cut open by someone who talks about a naughty appendix.

There was something else bothering him. It was the other doctor. Now where had he seen her before? He wished she were doing the operation. A lot of people smiled at the hospital but she was different – she looked as if she meant it.

"Mr Jones here is what we call the anaesthetist," said the Consultant when Jack arrived in another room. "He's going to give you a little prick in the arm and you'll fall asleep."

Was Jack dreaming already? The woman doctor had seemed to give him an enormous wink, as if they were old friends. As the anaesthetist bent over his arm, there was a familiar humming noise. The needle of the

injection suddenly bent over, like a wilting flower.

It couldn't be, could it? Jack looked at her more closely. The hair was different and she never used to have glasses, but there was something about the black nail varnish she was wearing. Now where had he seen black nail varnish?

"Funny," said the anaesthetist, reaching for another needle.

"A lot of funny things are happening in this hospital at the moment," said the Consultant. "Aren't they, Doctor Wisdom?"

Doctor Wisdom! It must be! She had promised she'd see him again. What were her exact words? "I go wherever magic is needed." He certainly needed magic now.

Jack felt the injection go into his arm. He heard a voice saying, "Now just count to three."

"Hi, Ms...Wiiiii..."

And Jack was fast asleep.

CHAPTER TWO
MAGIC ON FRIDAY

Hospitalised!

The word spread like wildfire through St Barnabas School the day after Jack was taken into hospital. The Morris twins, who knew the family that lived next door to him, said he would be away from school for days. By break time, the rumour was that he would miss the rest of term. By lunch, it was generally agreed that Jack was unlikely ever to be seen at school again.

"What's 'hospitalised', sir?" Caroline asked Mr Bailey during Class Five's first lesson.

"It means that someone has to go

16

into hospital," said the teacher, with
a sympathetic smile. "Why, Caroline?
Is it someone in your family?"

"It's Jack, sir. You remember that
pain he had, sir – in maths?"

"Jack?" Mr Bailey looked worried.
"I can't remember any pain."

"Siiir!" There were protests of
disbelief from around the classroom.

"Yes, yes, all right. I remember now."

"Well, it got worse and worse," said
Caroline, who was beginning to enjoy
herself now. "By the end of the day, he
was *screaming* in agony."

"Don't be ridiculous, Caroline," said
Mr Bailey nervously. "Er ... really?"

"Hospitalised," said Caroline
dramatically. She stared at Jack's
empty seat. "Apparently the doctors
only had one question. '*Why wasn't*

this child brought to us sooner?' There's going to be an investigation."

Mr Bailey had turned very pale.

"Um. Just got to visit the head teacher," he said, scurrying to the door with an anxious, hunted look. "Revise for your maths test, everyone. I'll be back in a minute."

*

The first time Jack woke up after his operation, he felt dizzy and sick. There was a tube sticking into his arm, he had a pain in his side, and his parents were talking at him.

Thinking that he almost preferred the stomach ache, he drifted off to sleep.

The second time Jack woke up after

his operation, it was evening and his parents had gone home, but Ms Wiz was standing beside his bed.

"Ms Wiz!" Jack said weakly.

"Dr Wisdom at your service. I thought you might be needing some special magic."

"Can you make me feel better?"

"I can't do that," said Ms Wiz, drawing the curtains around Jack's bed, "but I might be able to cheer you up a bit."

She reached into an inside pocket of her white coat and pulled out a china cat.

"Here's Hecate to look after you," she said, putting the cat on the bedside table. "Any time you need me, just tap her on the head."

"Thanks," croaked Jack.

"And you'll be needing some company," said Ms Wiz, putting her hand into another pocket and pulling out her tame, magic rat. "So Herbert will be staying with you until you're better."

She put Herbert the rat on to the bed. He sniffed around a bit and was about to scurry under the bedclothes when Ms Wiz said, "Not there, Herbert – it's unhygienic. Under the pillow."

"But—" Jack tried to concentrate. "How did you get here?"

"They were expecting a supply doctor, whom I happened to know was ill. So I just turned up. They're so desperate for doctors here that they never even asked to see my papers."

"Cool," said Jack.

"Now, remember," said Ms Wiz, tucking up the bed. "Don't tell any of the nurses or doctors about our secret. They may not like the idea of magic spells in a modern hospital. They might even think I'm a sort of witch."

"Can I tell the other children?"

Ms Wiz looked around the ward and smiled.

"Of course you can," she said.

"She's never a witch."

The boy in the bed next to Jack's was called Franklyn. He had a bad back and he didn't believe in magic.

"Witches are for wimps," he said.

There was a hiss from Hecate, the china cat, and her eyes lit up.

"Nice toy," said Franklyn,

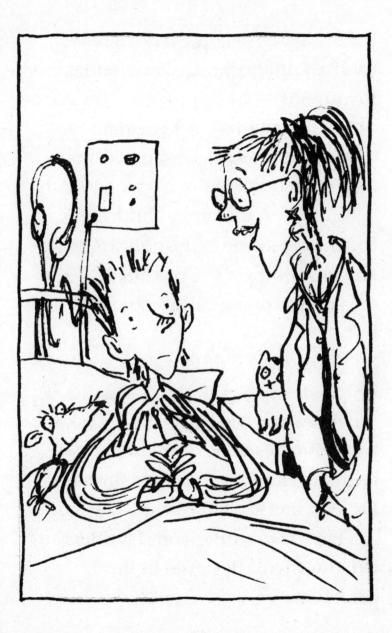

unimpressed. He picked up his football magazine and started leafing through it.

Jack was too tired to argue.

"Just you wait and see," he said.

The next morning, the children's ward was visited by the Consultant. There was a group of medical students with him.

"I took this young man's appendix out yesterday," said the Consultant, when he reached Jack's bed. He turned to Ms Wiz, who was standing at the back of the group. "How is he, Dr Wisdom?"

"He's recovering well," said Ms Wiz, with a little smile in Jack's direction.

The Consultant turned to the students and took a small bottle from his pocket.

"And here," he said, "is the appendix in question. As you can see it was badly inflamed."

The students looked at the bottle which seemed to contain a small red caterpillar, floating in liquid. The

Consultant put the bottle down on the table beside Jack's bed.

"Let's have a look at the patient," he said. "Miss Harris, would you like to check his heart?"

One of the students stepped forward, put a stethoscope to her ears and placed the other end on Jack's heart. There was a faint humming noise from the direction of Ms Wiz. The student looked puzzled.

"Well?" said the Consultant. "What do you hear?"

"It seems to be disco music," said the student.

Jack winked at Franklyn who was now unable to hide his curiosity.

"Give me that stethoscope," said the Consultant. He listened to Jack's heart. "Extraordinary," he said.

"Excuse me," said Franklyn from the next bed. "There's a..."

But the Consultant was too busy looking at the stethoscope in his hand to pay any attention.

Jack now saw what Franklyn was staring at. Herbert the rat had escaped from under his pillow and, using the bedspread as cover, had made his way down to the foot of the bed. As the

Consultant and his students examined the stethoscope, he peeped out, ran to where the little bottle containing Jack's appendix stood, picked it up in his mouth and scurried back under the bedclothes.

"Excuse me—" said Franklyn again.

Jack put a finger to his lips and shook his head slowly.

"Yes, Franklyn?" asked Ms Wiz innocently. "Is something the matter?"

"Er, maybe not," said Franklyn.

CHAPTER THREE
A VISIT ON SATURDAY

It was Saturday morning, Jack's third day without an appendix, and Caroline and Podge had been allowed by their parents to walk to the hospital to visit him.

"How you feeling, Jacko?" asked Podge.

"Not bad," said Jack. "Considering I've had a major operation."

"Major operation," sniffed Franklyn from the next bed. "All they did was take out a small, completely useless piece of gristle."

"Oh no!" Caroline looked shocked. "You mean it was a brain operation?"

Jack started to laugh, then clutched

his stomach. "Don't," he said. "It hurts when I laugh."

"I've got to admit that he's an interesting neighbour," Franklyn went on. "He thinks his doctor is a witch."

Podge looked amazed. "It's not...?"

"It is," smiled Jack.

"*And* he's got a rat under his pillow," Franklyn continued loudly.

"Sshh!" said Jack. "Don't let anyone know or there'll be trouble."

"Ah," said Franklyn. "Problem. I think I just did – about five minutes ago."

At that moment, there was a scream from the other end of the ward.

News travels fast in a hospital. Franklyn had told his other neighbour Katie, who was suffering from asthma. Katie had told Matthew,

who was hanging upside down
with two broken legs. Matthew
had told Michelle, who was having
tests. Michelle had told Amber, who
had just had her tonsils out. Amber
had whispered it to Tom, who had
grommets. Tom had told his mother
– and that was the scream from the
other end of the ward.

"Now children," said the Ward
Sister, as Tom's mother recovered on
a spare bed. "You may have heard
that a small, furry animal has been
seen in here..."

"She means a rat," said Franklyn.
There was a moan from Tom's mother.

"...and small, furry animals are not
welcome in hospitals, even if they are
pets. So the nurses are going to search
the ward."

"What will you do if you find it?" asked Jack.

"Confiscate it, of course," said the Ward Sister. "We're lucky enough to have an experimental laboratory downstairs. They always need fresh mice and rats."

Caroline and Podge gasped. Jack calmly leant over and tapped Hecate the cat's head. Her eyes flashed.

"Morning, Sister," said Ms Wiz, who breezed into the ward within seconds.

"Morning, Dr Wisdom."

Ms Wiz glanced at the nurses as they looked under the beds and in cupboards.

"Goodness," she said. "What's going on here?"

The Ward Sister whispered something in her ear.

"A *rat*?" Ms Wiz seemed shocked. "In that case, I'll just check the Beddows boy's dressing and leave you to it."

Ms Wiz hurried over to Jack's bed and pulled the curtains around it.

"Up to your old tricks, eh Ms Wiz?" said Caroline quietly.

"Just trying to cheer Jack up," said Ms Wiz, feeling under his pillow, eventually pulling out Herbert.

"Have you got one of those cardboard bottle things?" she asked Jack.

"You don't mean—?"

"That's right. The little bottles they give you to pee in when you're in bed."

Jack passed it to Ms Wiz, who had just slipped Herbert into the bottle when the curtains drew back. It was the Ward Sister.

"Jack's been a good boy, has he?" she said, looking at the bottle in Ms Wiz's hands.

"Er, yes."

"Allow me, Doctor," said the Ward Sister, taking the bottle. "I'll just get rid of this for you."

She was halfway across the ward when Herbert decided to put his head out for a quick look around. The Ward Sister shrieked and dropped the bottle.

"What on earth is going on?" The Consultant, who had heard the noise while passing, stood at the door. With a shaky hand, the Ward Sister pointed to Herbert who was coolly looking up at them.

"Stand back, everyone," shouted the Consultant, grabbing a long brush that was leaning against the wall. "Look away if you don't like the sight of squashed rodent."

He raised the brush over his head.

There was a humming noise from the direction of Ms Wiz.

Suddenly, the brush seemed to develop a life of its own. It leapt out of the Consultant's hands and pushed him towards an empty corner bed. As he fell back, the curtains drew around the bed. There were sounds of scuffling.

Not looking particularly alarmed, Herbert sidled down one side of the room and out of the door.

Ms Wiz held up her hands.

"Keep calm," she said. "The rat has

left the room. I'm sure he'll turn up—"
for a moment she looked worried
"—um, somewhere."

"Did you see that brush, Doctor?"
gasped the Ward Sister.

"I'm sure there's a perfectly logical
explanation for that," said Ms Wiz,
walking towards the door.

There were muffled sounds of
protest from the corner bed.

"What about the Consultant?" asked
the Ward Sister.

Ms Wiz drew back the curtains.
The Consultant was swathed head to
foot in bandages. He looked like an
Egyptian mummy.

"Let me out!" he gasped.
"Someone's going to pay for this!"

*

"Wow," said Franklyn, as the Consultant was wheeled out of the ward to have his bandages removed. "Your Ms Wiz is the strangest doctor I've ever seen."

"If it wasn't for you, Herbert wouldn't be wandering around the hospital," said Caroline.

"He'll be all right," said Jack. "After all, he's a magic rat."

Franklyn pulled the bedclothes up to his chin. "I'm not letting that Ms Wiz anywhere near me," he said. "She may be a good witch but I don't trust her as a doctor."

Caroline looked at her watch. "We'd better go, Podge," she said. "Remember we've got to revise for the maths test."

"Wait a minute," he said. "I want to

ask Jack a few more questions."

Jack sighed.

"This pain you had," said Podge. "Which side was it on?"

Podge appeared to be deep in thought. He had just had a rather brilliant idea.

CHAPTER FOUR
LUNCH ON SUNDAY

Mr Bailey was a worried man.

It was only his second year as a teacher and he was finding it very difficult. The children didn't seem to respect him somehow. Whatever he asked them to do, they did the opposite. They laughed at him behind his back. And they were always playing tricks on him.

That was what happened with Jack Beddows. He had been certain that Jack's stomach ache was just another trick. There was a big maths test on Monday and Jack hated maths.

But it wasn't. The stomach ache was real. Jack was in hospital and Mr

Bailey was in trouble.

Mr Gilbert, the head teacher at St Barnabas, had not been pleased when he heard what had happened.

"I take a dim view, Mr Bailey," he had said. "After all, children are people, you know."

"Are they?" Mr Bailey had said. He wasn't sure any more.

"Why not," the head teacher had sounded tired, "try to be nice for a change?"

"Yes, Mr Gilbert."

Which was why, this Sunday morning, Mr Bailey was going to visit the hospital. He had bought some flowers and a bunch of grapes and a Get Well card.

Maybe if he was nice to Jack, Class Five would be nice to him. It was worth a try.

Ms Wiz was worried too.

Ever since the Consultant had been pushed around by a brush and wrapped up like a Christmas present, he had been giving her very suspicious looks.

"It's strange," he said, as they did their morning rounds of the wards. "You turn up at the hospital as if by magic, and since then nothing's been quite normal. Bending needles, musical stethoscopes, flying brushes, rats. Where is that animal by the way?"

Ms Wiz shook her head. She hadn't the faintest idea where Herbert was. Secretly, she was afraid that he might decide to investigate the experimental laboratory. He could be quite a mischievous little rat sometimes.

"Yes, it is rather strange," she said.

"What's more, you're never around when real medical work is needed."

Ms Wiz laughed. "Perhaps that's a good thing," she said.

*

44

"Morning, nurse," said Jack's father to the Ward Sister as he arrived for his morning visit. "Has he been yet?"

"Dad!" protested Jack.

"Not yet," smiled the Ward Sister. "It takes a while after an appendix operation. Once he moves his bowels, we'll know he's really on the mend."

"What are bowels?" asked Jack's little sister Jenny.

"Things inside you that move from time to time," said Mrs Beddows.

"Not very often in Jack's case," boomed his father.

Jack noticed a familiar figure standing at the ward door, looking confused. At last, Mr Bailey spotted him.

"Hullo, young lad," he said. "I've brought you some goodies."

"Thank you," said Jack. "These are my parents and my sister. This is Mr Bailey."

The smile left the teacher's face.

"It...it wasn't my fault," he stammered. "They're always saying they've got stomach aches. Or ear aches. Or they feel sick. Particularly when there's a maths test coming up. You don't know who to believe, do

you? They're such liars, children.
I mean, not Jack – but the others...I
didn't know it was an appendix. I'm
not a doctor, am I? You can't blame me
for that...can you?"

"Don't worry, Mr Bailey," said
Jack's mother. "We all make mistakes."

There was an embarrassed silence.

"So," Jack said eventually. "Who'd
like to see my appendix?"

It was a tiring morning for Jack. Mr
Bailey always had that effect on him
and watching him trying to impress
his parents somehow made it even
worse. So, when a nurse brought him
lunch on a tray, he didn't feel the
slightest bit hungry.

"Come on, Jack," said his mother.

"You'll never get well if you don't eat."

"I just don't feel up to plastic chicken and stringy red cabbage," said Jack.

"Yum," said Mr Bailey loudly. "It looks delicious to me."

Quite why Ms Wiz walked into the ward at this particular moment, Jack never discovered. She was pretending to look at Tom, the boy with grommets, but Jack could tell that she was up to something from the quiet humming noise that was coming from her direction.

The bottle containing his appendix was on a table behind where Mr Bailey and his parents were sitting. This meant that only Jack and Franklyn saw the bottle open quietly.

As if it were a real, live caterpillar, the appendix wriggled out.

"Just eat a bit," Jack's father was saying. "A mouthful for each of us."

The appendix crawled along the edge of the table.

"It's getting cold," said his sister.

Jack was speechless. The appendix was making its way on to the lunch tray – and into the red cabbage.

"I know what we'll do," said Mr Bailey. "I'll eat a mouthful, then you eat a mouthful."

"I don't think—"

"Here's a spare spoon," interrupted Franklyn, with an innocent little smile.

"Er, Mr Bailey—" said Jack.

But it was too late. The teacher dipped his spoon into the red cabbage.

Jack closed his eyes. When he opened them, Mr Bailey was chewing with a slightly pained smile. The appendix had gone.

"Delicious," said Mr Bailey, swallowing with some difficulty.

Jack glanced over to where Ms Wiz was standing. He really thought she had gone too far this time. She shrugged helplessly.

"That's odd," said Franklyn, pointing at the empty appendix bottle. "Your spare part's gone missing."

"So it has," said Jack.

"Funny how similar to red cabbage it looks," said Franklyn.

Mr Bailey looked at the empty bottle and then at the half-eaten plate of cabbage. Suddenly he felt a little queasy.

"Better be going now," he said, getting unsteadily to his feet.

"Bye, sir," said Jack. "Thanks for coming."

Mr Bailey walked quickly out of the hospital towards his car. It couldn't have been, could it? That red cabbage *had* tasted a little rubbery.

Perhaps the story would get out. Jack would be bound to spread it around. It would probably get into the local paper. He could see the headlines now. "CRUEL TEACHER EATS BOY'S APPENDIX."

"Why me?" he shouted to an empty car park. He kicked his car, hurting his foot. "Why is it always me?"

CHAPTER FIVE
MAYHEM ON MONDAY

Ms Wiz had looked everywhere for
Herbert. She had visited all the wards
in the hospital. She had checked in the
reception hall. She had even searched
the kitchen. The only place where she
had yet to look was the experimental
laboratory, which had been locked up
over the weekend.

Now it was Monday morning
and Ms Wiz was on her way to the
laboratory. It was her last chance.
After all, life wouldn't be the same
without Herbert.

"Dr Wisdom!"

Ms Wiz heard a familiar voice
behind her as she hurried down a

corridor. She turned to see the
Consultant.

"Where are you going?" he asked.

"I was just looking in on the
laboratory," said Ms Wiz. "Er, I'm
rather interested in an experiment
they're doing."

"You're looking for that rat, aren't
you?"

"Rat?"

"You know what I think?" The
Consultant put his face close to hers.
"I don't think you're a doctor at all.
I've seen the way you go pale at the
sight of blood. You're never around
when I need help with an operation.
I think you're an intruder."

Ms Wiz smiled. She was wondering
whether she should turn him into a
rabbit. Perhaps not, she decided. A
rabbit hopping about the hospital with
a stethoscope around its neck would
make people even more suspicious.

"I'm going to check your papers,"
said the Consultant. "If it turns out
you're not a real doctor, I'm calling the
police. Impersonating a doctor – that's
serious." He smiled coldly. "They'll
probably send you to prison."

*

Jack was sitting on the edge of his bed. Although his stomach was still sore and he was a bit weak, he was feeling much better. His parents were going to take him home that morning.

"So it's goodbye again," said Ms Wiz, who was doing her normal round of the children's ward. "Your stitches will come out in a few days' time and you'll be as good as new."

"Thank you for looking after me," said Jack. "Having an appendix out isn't so bad after all."

"I think you should go and see Mr Bailey as soon as you can," said Ms Wiz. "After all, he visited you."

"Do us some more tricks, Doc," said Franklyn. "I'm going out tomorrow and I'll have something to tell them."

"No more tricks, I'm afraid,

Franklyn. I'm leaving today."

"What about Herbert?" asked Jack.

"He'll just have to look after himself," said Ms Wiz. "I can't find him anywhere."

Just then, the doors of the ward opened and the Consultant strode in, his white coat flapping. There were two policemen with him.

"That's her!" he said, pointing at Ms Wiz. "She's the imposter."

"But that's Dr Wisdom," said the Ward Sister.

"Doctor? Hah!" The Consultant's voice echoed round the children's ward as the two policemen advanced towards Ms Wiz.

One of them, who had now produced a notebook, asked, "Are you Doctor, or Miss Dolores Wis—?"

At that moment, the swing doors behind the Consultant crashed open and a white tidal wave of live, squeaking creatures poured into the ward.

"What on earth—?" gasped the Consultant.

Mice! Hundreds of them, swarming around the floor, climbing the curtains, exploring every corner. And, in the thick of them, standing up on his hind legs and looking about him, like a general surveying the field of battle, was Herbert.

"There you are, Herbert," said Ms Wiz, reaching down for him. "So you were in the laboratory, after all, were you? Freeing all the mice."

Jack picked his way through the swarm of white mice and whispered something in the Consultant's ear.

"Dr Wisdom," the Consultant shouted over the din. "Rid the hospital of these creatures and you can go free – I'll drop all charges against you."

Ms Wiz raised her hand and whistled. The mice froze, staring at her with little pink eyes. She picked up Herbert and looked around the ward for the last time.

"Thanks, Jack," she said cheerfully. "See you again soon."

"And me, Ms Wiz," said Franklyn.

"Of course. Whenever a bit of magic's needed. Bye everyone." She waved to the other children before making her way out of the ward, followed by Herbert's mouse army.

*

"And so Ms Wiz saved the hospital from a plague of white mice," Jack told Class Five that afternoon when he visited them. Even Mr Bailey, who had allowed Jack to speak about hospital during a lesson, looked impressed.

"What will she do with the mice?" asked Caroline.

"Probably lead them to the countryside and set them free," said Jack.

Alex put his hand up. "Can we see your appendix?" he asked. "Caroline said you'd kept it in a bottle."

"Right, back to work, class," Mr Bailey interrupted nervously.

"Oh, I threw it away," said Jack. "Who wants an old piece of gristle anyway?"

He glanced at Mr Bailey, who smiled with relief. Perhaps the head teacher had been right. Children were humans, after all.

"By the way," asked Jack. "Where's Podge?"

An ambulance raced through the streets of the town, its siren blaring and its blue light flashing.

In the back lay the patient, moaning quietly and clutching his right side.

"It worked!" thought Podge, as the ambulance screeched around a corner. He had remembered everything Jack had told him about the appendix, Mr Bailey had called the doctor, and here he was on the way to hospital. All he would have now was a small

operation, five days in hospital with
Ms Wiz looking after him, a few
stitches and that would be that. It was
a small price to pay for missing the
maths test.

The ambulance stopped. The doors
were opened and Podge was wheeled
on a stretcher towards the hospital.

"Hullo, Podge." It was Ms Wiz, with
Hecate under her arm. "What's up?"

"Appendix, Ms Wiz," groaned Podge.

Hecate's eyes lit up.

"Oh dear. What a pity I'm just going," said Ms Wiz. "In fact, I only came back to collect Hecate."

"Going?"

"So you'll just have to face your major operation all on your own."

Podge gulped. "Er, maybe..."

Ms Wiz laughed. "Lend us your stretcher, Podge," she said.

Podge thought for a moment, and then rolled off the stretcher.

"Oh well," he said. "It was worth a try."

"Thanks, Podge," said Ms Wiz, climbing on. The stretcher rose and hovered over the heads of the ambulance men.

"I'll be back – when you're least
expecting me," she called out as the
stretcher rose higher, turned slowly
and floated over the roof of the
hospital and out of sight.

As Podge and the ambulance men
watched Ms Wiz disappear, a nurse
walked out of the hospital. She had a
clipboard under her arm.

"Well, young man," she said. "Let's get you registered. How's the pain now?"

"Better, thank you," said Podge. "Suddenly much better."

IN CONTROL,
Ms Wiz?

CHAPTER ONE

"WHO WAS THAT WOMAN?"

Above Mr Goff's desk at the Latimer Road Library was a sign which read "QUIET, PLEASE!" Today, as usual, it was being ignored.

In the children's corner, a group of five-year-olds were laughing at a story being read to them by their teacher.

By one of the armchairs, a bluebottle was buzzing around the head of an old man who had fallen asleep.

Among the bookshelves, the new assistant librarian was flicking her duster at the books like a charioteer cracking a whip.

At the front desk, Mr Goff was sniffling into his handkerchief.

And, in the reference section, Peter Harris – "Podge" to everyone who knew him – was telling his school friend Jack Beddows some really interesting facts he had just discovered.

"Did you know that in 1955, Phillip Yadzik of Chicago, USA, ate 77 large hamburgers in two hours?"

"Gross," said Jack, who was trying to read a football book.

"Or that the heaviest man in the world came from East Ham, England, and weighed an astonishing 59 stone?"

"Mmm, big," said Jack.

"And that the world's largest jelly—"

"Podge," said Jack, putting down his book. "Did you know that the most annoying person in the entire universe is Podge 'Motormouth'

Harris of London, England, who once had a *Guinness Book of Records* pushed right up his left nostril because he talked about food all the time?"

"All right, all right," said Podge. "I was just trying to improve your general knowledge."

At that moment, the sniffling noise coming from Mr Goff's desk stopped. He took a deep breath and went, "Wah-wah-wah-WAAHHH!"

It was an extraordinary noise for anyone to make and it was particularly strange coming from Mr Goff, who was a timid, polite man. Normally, the only sound he ever made was the occasional "Sssshhh!"

Everybody stared. Mr Goff removed his spectacles and wiped them with a handkerchief. He looked around the library, sniffed a few times and took another deep breath.

"WAAAAHHHHHH!"

"Fire!" said the old man in the armchair, waking up with a start. "Don't panic! I heard the siren! Pensioners out first!"

"Podge," said Jack out of the side of his mouth. "I think the librarian is crying."

"How embarrassing," said Podge.

The teacher who had been reading to the children walked over to the front desk.

"Are you all right, Mr Goff?" she asked.

The librarian sniffed miserably.

"Perhaps it's hay fever," said the old man, who had now realised that

the noise which had woken him was
not a fire alarm.

Podge and Jack joined the group
now standing around the front desk.
They felt sorry for Mr Goff but,
not being used to grown librarians
bursting into tears in the middle of the
day, they couldn't think of anything to
say.

The new assistant librarian, a
young woman with her dark hair in a
ponytail, went round to the other side
of the desk and put her arm around
Mr Goff.

"Cheer up," she said. "It might
never happen."

"It already has," said the librarian
miserably. He gave her the sheet of
paper that he had been reading. "Look
at this note from the council."

"*Notice of closure*," the assistant librarian read out. "*The council gives notice that, as from the end of this month, the Latimer Road Library will be closed—*"

"Oh dear," said the teacher.

"*—and that all the books will be transferred to the nearby St Edward's Road Library—*"

"Nearby?" said the old man. "It's too far for me to walk to."

"The library staff will be given jobs in another library. Signed, The Chief Leisure Officer."

"I don't want a job in another library," said Mr Goff, his voice cracking as if he were about to cry again. The teacher put her arm around his shoulders.

"There, there," she said.

"Jack," said Podge, looking closely at the assistant librarian, who was now taking off her nylon cleaning coat. "Does she remind you of someone?"

"Yes, she does," said Jack. "But what on earth is she doing here?"

The assistant librarian briskly peeled off the gloves in which she had been dusting the shelves. Standing there in her purple T-shirt and jeans, she looked quite different.

"It must be her," said Podge. "Who else would wear black nail varnish to work in a library?"

"That's enough talk," said the assistant librarian with her hands on her hips. "It's time for action. The end of the month – that means they'll be closing the library on Friday, unless we can stop them. Jack, Podge – I'll need your help. Now here's what we're going to do..."

Jack and Podge exchanged glances. She knew their names. "Here we go again," said Podge with a smile.

A few minutes later, the assistant librarian gathered up her belongings and strode out of the library, saying she had some spells to prepare.

"Spells?" said the teacher after she had left. "What's going on?"

"Yes, who *was* that woman in the purple T-shirt?" asked Mr Goff.

"That was Ms Wiz," said Podge.

"If anyone can save the library," said Jack, "Ms Wiz can. She has magic on her side."

"Good old Ms Wiz," said Mr Goff. He didn't seem convinced.

"Dad," said Podge that evening, as the Harris family ate dinner. "Is it true that the council wants to close the library?"

"It is," said Mr Harris, who was a councillor. "There are too many libraries in this area. We're selling it to make flats." He stabbed a sausage

with his fork. "Very nice flats they'll
be too."

"What about the people who use the
library?" asked Podge. "They matter
too."

"Don't be cheeky to your father,"
said Mrs Harris.

"It's true," Podge insisted. "People
need that library. And—" Podge
lowered his voice, "—Ms Wiz is going
to save it."

"Did you say Wiz? Is that Wiz
woman getting involved?" Mr Harris
looked worried. He remembered
last term at St Barnabas when an
owl taught maths, a school inspector
found a rat in his trousers and two
of the teachers were turned into
geese. "That woman spells
trouble."

"*Someone*'s got to save our books for us," said Podge.

Mr Harris dipped his sausage into some tomato sauce.

"Remember this, son," he said solemnly. "Books are books – and business is business. And never the twain shall meet. Am I right, Mum?"

"You certainly are, Dad," said Mrs Harris.

CHAPTER TWO
"IS THIS A LIBRARY OR A ZOO?"

That Friday afternoon, Jack and Podge met in the park and set off for Latimer Road Library. Jack brought his skateboard, because he took his skateboard everywhere, and Podge brought a large box of sandwiches, just in case saving the library carried on over tea-time.

But when they arrived at Latimer Road, they received a shock. The library was closed and Mr Goff was sitting on the steps outside, looking miserable.

"They've locked it up," he said. "My own library and I can't get in."

"That's strange," said Jack. "It

wasn't meant to be closed until tonight."

"Maybe the Chief Leisure Officer heard that your Ms Wiz had magic on her mind," said Mr Goff.

"But how?" Jack was puzzled. "It was meant to be a secret. No one would be stupid enough to blab to someone on the council, would they?"

"Well..." Podge was looking as if he wished he were somewhere else.

"Oh no," said Jack. "You didn't mention it to your father, did you?"

"You see—"

"Podge," said Jack wearily. "You are a complete and utter nerdbrain."

"Perhaps Ms Wiz will know what to do," said Podge weakly.

Mr Goff sniffed. "If she turns up."

"She'll be here soon," said Jack.

"She'll probably fly in on her vacuum cleaner."

"Or just appear out of thin air," said Podge.

At that moment, the number 22 bus drew up in front of the library. Ms Wiz stepped out, carrying a plastic bag.

"Huh," said Mr Goff. "Some witch."

Ms Wiz was against giving up and

going home (Mr Goff's suggestion), or smashing the door down (Jack's suggestion), or discussing the whole thing over a few sandwiches and cakes (Podge's suggestion).

"The people from the council will be here soon," she said. "After all, no one has told Mr Goff what's going to happen to him."

"What do we do when they get here?" asked Mr Goff.

"We magic 'em," said Podge with a grin.

"Yeah," said Jack. "Ms Wiz will use Hecate, the china cat with flashing eyes, Archie the owl and Herbert the magic rat."

"Oh, whoops!" Ms Wiz clapped a hand to her forehead. "I left them all at home."

Mr Goff, Jack and Podge looked at her in amazement.

"All right," she said with a shrug. "Nobody's perfect."

"Well, what *have* you got?" asked Jack, beginning to wonder whether Ms Wiz was a bit less magic than she used to be.

Ms Wiz looked inside her plastic

bag and eventually brought out a small bottle the size of a pepperpot.

"I've got some Fish Powder," she said.

"Great," said Podge. "We can sprinkle it on my sandwiches. Fish and peanut butter. Yummy."

"And how," asked Mr Goff, "is fish powder going to save a library?"

"This is special Fish Powder," said Ms Wiz. "All we need are some books." She walked briskly towards the library door. "Ah," she said, suddenly remembering that it was locked.

"It's not your day, is it?" said Mr Goff.

Ms Wiz ignored him. "Jack," she said, "have you got any books on you?"

"Nothing much," muttered Jack. "Just a few by Beatrix Potter."

"Beatrix Potter?" Podge started to laugh. "Beatrix *Potter*?"

Jack blushed. "They were for my sister," he said.

"Oh no," said Mr Goff, as a car drew up. "Here comes Mrs Prescott, the Chief Leisure Officer."

"Quick!" shouted Ms Wiz. "Give me those books."

Jack pulled a number of small books from his jacket pocket. Ms Wiz laid them on the ground, as the Chief Leisure Officer approached.

"If you close this library down," Ms Wiz called out, reaching for her bottle of Fish Powder, "I shall not be answerable for the consequences."

"This is no longer a library," said

Mrs Prescott. "It's merely a room with books in it. We shall soon remove the books so that it can be converted into flats."

"I warned you," said Ms Wiz, opening the Beatrix Potter books and sprinkling Fish Powder on their pages. There was a slight humming sound, which could be heard above the noise of the traffic on Latimer Road. Then, one by one, a succession of small animals, wearing waistcoats and pinafores, came to life and hopped out of the pages of the books and on to the pavement.

Soon Pigling Bland, the Fierce Bad Rabbit, Jemima Puddle-Duck, Peter Rabbit and several Flopsy Bunnies were hopping, waddling and scurrying about in front of the library.

"Wicked, Ms Wiz," said Jack.

"What's going on?" said Mrs Prescott. "Is this a library or a zoo?"

"This Fish Powder," said Ms Wiz, "can bring any character in a book to life." Jemima Puddle-Duck was wandering off, causing quite a stir outside the newsagent. "We can bring

total confusion to this area unless you leave us our library."

"Fish Powder?" said Mrs Prescott, stepping carefully over the Fierce Bad Rabbit.

"Right," said Ms Wiz. "FISH stands for Freeing Illustrated Storybook Heroes. It's a magic potion."

Podge and Jack gave a cheer.

Ms Wiz held up her hand. "If you don't leave this library alone, I'll release more characters. I can bring this road to a standstill."

"You won't get away with this," said Mrs Prescott, backing towards her car and nearly falling over a Flopsy Bunny in the process. "We'll be back."

She drove off quickly.

"Now," said Ms Wiz. "Let's get these animals under control."

Just then, there was a squeal of brakes from the road behind them.

"Oh no," said Podge. "That's the number 66 bus. I don't think the driver saw one of our animals."

"It's Peter Rabbit!" gasped Jack.

"Peter Rabbit? Under a bus?" Mr Goff had gone pale. "But this could change the whole shape of children's literature."

"It's certainly changed the shape of Peter Rabbit," said Podge, looking into the road.

"He was my favourite," wailed Jack.

"Don't worry," said Ms Wiz. "The Fish Powder will sort him out." She took a deep breath, sprinkled some powder on the pages of *The Tale of Peter Rabbit* and shouted, "HSIF REDWOP!"

The shape in the middle of the road disappeared. Jack looked inside his book.

"Phew!" he said. "Peter's back."

"I thought those books were for your sister," said Podge.

"Never mind that," said Ms Wiz. "We're not going to be able to change

the council's mind with a few Flopsy
Bunnies. What other books have you
got?"

Podge reached inside his lunchbox.
"How about this?" he said.

CHAPTER THREE
"WHERE EXACTLY DID YOU MEET HIM, PETER?"

Mr and Mrs Harris were watching television. This was one of their favourite ways of passing the time, and Mr Harris even used to sneak home on Friday afternoons to watch *The Avenue*, the soap opera he liked most of all.

"That Maylene's heading for trouble," he said to Mrs Harris, as he sipped his tea, waiting for *The Avenue* to begin. "She shouldn't be going out with that dentist when she's already engaged to the schoolteacher."

"No," said Mrs Harris. "Not after what happened at the barbecue."

"Where's the boy?"

For a moment, Mrs Harris thought her husband was still talking about the dentist. Then she realized he meant Peter, their son.

"Down at the library," she said. "Nose in a book as usual."

"Books!" said Podge's father. "Who needs books? When I was his age, I didn't go filling my head with things from books. It never did me any harm. Turn the telly up, Mum."

Mrs Harris turned up the volume on the television.

"Anyway," shouted Mr Harris. "We closed that library today."

"And now—" said the television announcer, '—it's time to visit *The Avenue*."

The front doorbell rang.

"That'll be Peter," said Mr Harris. He got up, grumbling. "If the bell goes at an awkward time when everyone's busy—" he opened the front door, "— it's always...er, good afternoon."

There, on the doorstep, was the fattest man Mr Harris had ever seen. He was wearing Bermuda shorts and a baseball cap.

"Can I help you?" asked Mr Harris nervously.

The man pointed to his mouth.

"Hi, dad," said Podge, jumping out from behind the giant. "This is my friend Phillip Yadzik of Chicago, USA."

Mr Harris smiled. "Howdeedodee, Phillip," he said.

"He's rather hungry," said Podge. "He's been in *The Guinness Book of Records* for the last few years."

"Well, he would be," said Mr Harris, looking puzzled.

Yadzik squeezed his way through the front door. Once inside the house, he sniffed the air like a dog at dinner-time.

"Would you like to watch *The Avenue*?" asked Mr Harris weakly. "It's just started."

"I think," said Podge, "he'd rather have a bite to eat."

Yadzik pushed his way past Mr Harris and made for the kitchen. He opened the fridge and gulped down three chicken pies, two dozen sausages and a family box of chips, complete with plastic wrapping.

"Is that Peter with one of his friends?" Mrs Harris called out from next door.

"That's right, Mum," said Podge.

Yadzik was just swallowing a large white loaf of bread, when Podge's mother came out to meet him.

"Oh!" she said. Trying to look normal when a giant is eating his way through your kitchen isn't easy, but somehow Mrs Harris remembered her manners. "What a big boy you are," she said. "Do you go to Peter's school?"

"He doesn't talk," said Podge. "Apparently characters freed from books can't talk. The words belong to their authors."

"I see," said Mrs Harris, who didn't see at all. "Where exactly did you meet him, Peter?"

"In the Food and Gluttony section of *The Guinness Book of Records*. Back in 1955, he ate 77 large hamburgers in two hours. In 1957, he got through 101 bananas in fifteen minutes. But he hasn't eaten for several years, so those records are probably about to be broken."

"Our Sunday lunch," squealed Mrs Harris, as Yadzik found a chicken in the freezer and, with a great crunching noise, sank his teeth into it.

"I don't think he can wait until Sunday," said Podge.

"He's going to eat us out of house and home," said Mr Harris. "Tell him to go away, Peter – please."

"Oh dear," said Podge. "He's going into the front room. I wonder what he'll eat there."

Yadzik sat down heavily on the sofa, breaking all its legs. He casually reached for a cushion and started eating at it.

"He may eat you out of house and home," said Podge casually. "But he'll probably eat the house and home first."

"What are we going to do?" said Mr Harris. Podge had never seen his father look so helpless before.

"The thing is," he answered, as Yadzik tore down a curtain and began chewing one end. "Phillip used to be just a picture in a book. That was his home."

"Yeees?" said Mr Harris, looking puzzled.

"And now someone is closing down the library, where his book was kept. It's the Latimer Road Library."

"Go on," said Mr Harris suspiciously.

"So if someone could just *open* the library," Podge continued, "I'm sure Phillip would be happy to go home. In fact, Ms Wiz just has to sprinkle some powder on his pages and say some funny words and he'll be back in the book, just another weird record."

"Ms Wiz!" said Mr Harris. "I might have known that she'd be involved."

There was a cracking noise as Yadzik crushed a table and started picking at the legs like a smaller person might eat chips.

"I'll ring Mrs Prescott," said Mr Harris, picking up the phone and dialling. "Try and distract him with the television, Mum."

"I wouldn't do that," said Podge.

"Hullo," said Mr Harris into the telephone. "Is that Mrs Prescott, the Chief Leisure Officer? This is Councillor Cuthbert Harris. I want you to open the Latimer Road Library. Yes, this afternoon. It's an emergency."

"Now, Phillip," Mrs Harris was saying. "How about a bit of television?"

"I really don't think that's a good idea," said Podge.

The giant looked at Mrs Harris for a moment. Then his eyes shifted to the television and he smiled.

"No, I'm not drunk," Mr Harris was shouting into the phone. "This Ms Wiz is releasing characters from books. They're everywhere! Hullo? Mrs Prescott? Are you there?"

Yadzik walked over to the television, took out the plug and picked it up with a hungry grunt. He licked his lips.

"Not the television!" screamed Mr Harris, dropping the phone. "You can eat anything but that! NOOOOOOOO!"

CHAPTER FOUR
"PWOBLEM?"

"Um..."

Mr Goff had never been a very brave man. In fact, he was extremely nervous. That was why he had become a librarian. Books were easier to deal with than people. They didn't answer back, or make a noise, or call you names behind your back.

"Um, excuse me..."

That is, until Ms Wiz came along with her Fish Powder. It was all very well saving the library by Freeing Illustrated Storybook Characters, but once people from books started walking about the place, living their own lives, where would it all end?

"Um, excuse me, I say..."

In trouble. That's where it would end. Mr Goff tried to imagine what Latimer Road Library would be like, if this Fish Powder was being scattered about. Ms Wiz had said that they couldn't talk when they were outside the pages of their books, but what would happen if someone brought *The History of the Second World War* to life?

Or *Great Whales of the World*? Or – a terrible thought occurred to him – the rude pictures in some of the Sunday papers? It would cause a riot.

"Um, excuse me, I say, would you mind listening...?"

Ms Wiz, Jack and Podge continued to ignore Mr Goff as, standing outside the library, they discussed what to do next.

"SSSSHHHH!"

At last, they all turned round and noticed that the librarian was trying to say something.

"It seems to me," said Mr Goff, "that this is all getting a bit out of control."

"Not really," said Podge. "Peter Rabbit's back in his book. Ms Wiz returned Phillip to Food and Gluttony by sprinkling Fish Powder on his lines and saying 'HSIF REDWOP' before he ate my house. Shame about the television, though."

"Don't you want to save your library?" asked Jack.

"Of course, I do," said Mr Goff. "But are squashed rabbits and hamburger-crazed Americans really going to help us? Mrs Prescott will simply call the police and that will be that."

"I suppose you're right," said Ms Wiz.

"We need to change Mrs Prescott's mind somehow," said Mr Goff.

"I don't know how," said Ms Wiz. "The library's closed and we haven't got any more books to bring to life."

"Unless—" Mr Goff looked more embarrassed than ever as he reached into his briefcase "—you can use this."

He gave a picture book to Ms Wiz.

"Well done, Mr Goff," she said smiling.

"I was always a bit of a fan of their majesties," he said.

Podge looked at the book.

"I don't get it," he said. "How on earth can *The Bumper Book of Royal Weddings* help us?"

When Caroline Smith received a telephone call from her friend Jack, asking for her help, she wasn't a bit surprised.

"Not homework again?" she said.

"We need someone who can do voices," said Jack. "You're the best actress I know. See you at the Town Hall in ten minutes."

"Hang on," said Caroline. "Who's we?"

"Me, Podge – and Ms Wiz."

Caroline gave a little whoop of delight. "I'll be there," she said.

It had been a very normal day for Mrs Prescott, the Chief Leisure Officer. The only interesting thing to happen was a rather odd call from Cuthbert Harris –

something about the Latimer Road Library and his television being eaten – which she had ignored. Cuthbert sometimes enjoyed a drink or three at lunchtime. It was probably his idea of a joke.

There was a knock at the door.

"Come in," said Mrs Prescott.

"I...but...if...sir...help..." It was her secretary Mrs Simpson, who seemed to be having trouble speaking.

"What on *earth* is the matter, Mrs Simpson?"

"Wheah is the Chief Lejaah Orficer?" said a loud voice from next door. "I *demaaaand* to see her!"

The door burst open to reveal the most unusual visitors Mrs Prescott had ever received.

"It's their Royal Highnesses," said

113

Mrs Simpson, recovering her voice at last. "A famous prince and princess from Buckingham Palace. They're making a surprise visit to the Town Hall."

"We're gaying walkabout, aaahn't we, deah?" said the voice coming from the princess.

"Don't overdo the accent," Jack whispered to Caroline as they stood, with Podge, Ms Wiz and Mr Goff, behind the royal couple. It was lucky, he thought, that the princess was in her wedding dress and wore a veil over her face. No one could see that her mouth wasn't moving with Caroline's words.

"Are you the Chief Lejaah Orficer?"

"Yes, ma'am." Mrs Prescott was hurriedly tidying the papers on her desk, while trying to curtsey at the same time. "At your service, ma'am."

The prince, smiling his royal smile, shook her hand.

"Tell meah, may good womaaan," continued Caroline in her princess voice. "How is may favouwite libway, the Latimaaah Woad Libway? Ay *love* weading."

Mrs Prescott winced. "It's c-c-c-closed," she said eventually.

"AY BIG YOUR PAAAHDON?"

"We...I've just closed it down, ma'am."

"May favouwite libway? I wed may vair farst book theah."

Mrs Prescott looked confused.

"I think," said Jack helpfully, "that Her Royal Highness is saying that she read her very first book there."

"Yah," said Caroline.

"Did you, ma'am?" Mrs Prescott was unable to hide her surprise. Somehow the princess didn't look as if she came from the Latimer Road area.

"Ay *demaaaand* that you aypen it. This vair afternoon."

Mrs Prescott gulped.

"We can't aypen – I mean open it," she said. "We've only just closed it. It would be a problem."

"PWOBLEM?" Caroline's voice hit a new high note. "Well, if you can't aypen it, we jolly well shall. Shaaan't we, Pwincey?"

The prince was still smiling his royal smile and shaking hands with everyone. He now stood where Caroline was crouched behind the

princess. He smiled and held out his hand.

"Leave off, prince," muttered Podge. "I think she's a bit busy at present."

"Ay'm gaying theah wight now," said Caroline. "Ay maight even mention you in may speech when ay aypen the libway."

"Speech?" said Jack under his breath. "I don't believe it."

"Thank you, ma'am." Mrs Prescott

gave a little bob of the head.

"So the Latimah Woad Libway will be aypen again, awight? And stay aypen, OK?"

"Yes, Your Royal Highness," said Mrs Prescott.

"Yeah!" said Jack, rather too loudly.

Mrs Prescott looked up sharply.

"Sorry, ma'am, did you say something?"

"Yah," said Caroline quickly. "OK, yah."

"Ma'am," said Mrs Prescott, blushing. "May I ask Your Royal Highness why you appear to be wearing your wedding dress."

There was a moment's pause.

"Because...Ectually..." Caroline was thinking fast. "Because it's may anniverseway. So theah!"

And with that, the royal couple, followed by Caroline, Jack, Podge, Mr Goff and Ms Wiz, swept out of the room.

CHAPTER FIVE

"FRANKENSTEIN COMES TO LATIMER ROAD"

It took quite a long time for the royal party to walk from the Town Hall to Latimer Road because the prince insisted on shaking hands with everyone they met.

"May wedding dwess is getting dusty," said Caroline at one point. "Could you be bwidesmaid and pick it up for me, Podge?"

"You must be joking," said Podge. "Anyway what are you going to say in your speech?"

Caroline laughed. "Ay'll think of something," she said.

A few steps behind them, Mr Goff

was walking with Ms Wiz.

"I can't help noticing," he said, "that you don't seem to be your normal happy self."

Ms Wiz sighed. "You were right, Mr Goff," she said. "It's not my day."

"But why not? The library's going to be re-opened."

"If I tell you something, will you promise not to panic?"

Mr Goff nodded.

"I've lost the Fish Powder. I think someone's taken it."

"Oh dear." Mr Goff started panicking. For some reason, he started thinking about the Second World War. Great Whales of the World. The rude pictures in the Sunday papers. "Oh *dear*!" he said.

By the time the royal couple had

reached Latimer Road, there was quite a crowd following them. Waiting for them at the library was Mrs Prescott, who had driven there as quickly as possible and hung a pink ribbon across the doorway.

"Your Highnesses *walked*?" she said with disbelief in her voice.

Caroline crouched down behind the princess once more.

"We laik to meet the common people," she said loudly.

"Common?" said Jack. "That's nice."

Mrs Prescott gave the princess a pair of scissors.

"If you would be so kind as to cut the ribbon, Your Highness," she said, "we can then open the library."

The princess took the scissors. Behind her, Caroline shouted, "Thenks

to the efforts of your soopah Chief
Lejaah Orficer Mrs Prescott, and to
your divaine libwawian Mr Goff, not
to mention the absolutely spiffing Ms
Wiz, ay can declare this libway well
and twuly aypen!"

Everyone cheered as the princess
cut the ribbon and, closely followed by
her prince and Caroline, walked into
the library.

Soon the place was as busy as ever.
The princess sat down with a group
of five-year-olds who were being read
a story. The prince shook hands with
the old man who was settling back
into his favourite armchair.

"Ms Wiz," said Podge. "I think it's
Fish Powder time. If you don't return
the prince and princess to their book
soon, Mrs Prescott's going to get

suspicious. Caroline can't keep that voice up much longer."

"Now where *is* that Fish Powder?" said Ms Wiz, rummaging in her plastic bag. "It could really be most embarrassing if it fell into the wrong hands."

Just then a woman fainted at the far end of the library. Standing next to her, looking slightly confused, was a ghost.

"Where has Jack got to?" Ms Wiz asked suddenly.

Podge shrugged. "I think I saw him in the Horror and Ghost section," he said.

"And where's that?"

"Behind where that monster with three heads has just appeared out of thin air."

"*Oh no!*" said Ms Wiz.

Soon the library was in total confusion, with spirits, zombies, werewolves and vampires wandering in and out of the shelves. There were screams of alarm as men, women and children stampeded towards the door. Even the prince and princess looked rather surprised.

"Wow," said Podge. "Frankenstein comes to Latimer Road."

"It's all right," Ms Wiz was shouting. "They can't harm you. They're not real, I promise!"

But no one listened to her.

"Sorreee," said Jack, ambling up to her with the bottle of Fish Powder in his hand. "I just wanted to see if it worked."

Without a word, Ms Wiz took the

bottle and sprinkled powder over the pages Jack had opened.

"HSIF REDWOP!" she shouted. "HSIF REDWOP!"

Gradually, the library was cleared as the demons returned to the books from which they had come.

"I've seen everything now," said Mrs Prescott, who had turned quite white. "A royal visit, then Frankenstein in Latimer Road. I'm glad I don't work here."

"So you won't close us again?" asked Mr Goff.

"Certainly not," said Mrs Prescott, backing out of the door. "This is your library, Mr Goff – and you're welcome to it. Goodbye."

Mr Goff turned to Ms Wiz. "Could I have my *Bumper Book of Royal Weddings* back now?" he asked.

"Of course," said Ms Wiz. "Let me just put the royal couple back." She sprinkled some Fish Powder on to the book and said, "HSIF REDWOP."

The prince and princess started to fade. The last Jack, Podge and Caroline saw of them was a royal smile.

"What a charming couple," said Ms Wiz, giving Mr Goff back his book. "Now, I'd better be off myself."

"Can't you stay?" said Mr Goff.

"The library won't be the same without you."

"Of course it will," said Ms Wiz. "You're the best librarian I've ever met."

Mr Goff blushed.

"Anyway," said Caroline. "Ms Wiz always comes back. She goes wherever magic's needed."

"That's right, Caroline," said Ms Wiz. "Cheerio, everyone."

She held the bottle of Fish Powder high in the air and tapped some out on to her head. "HSIF REDWOP," she said. She smiled, gave a little wave – and faded away.

For the first time in Mr Goff's memory, there was complete silence in the library.

"Whaaaaat?" said Podge eventually. "That means that Ms Wiz is a character in a story."

There was another silence.

"And if she comes from a book," said Caroline, "then where does that leave us?"

"Don't even *think* about it," said Jack.

ABOUT THE AUTHOR

Terence Blacker is a highly respected writer of both adult novels and children's fiction. He has a weekly column for the *Independent*, and is a regular broadcaster. His childhood ambition was to be a champion steeplechase jockey, but although he did try it after university, he rapidly moved on to bookselling, publishing, and finally found his vocation as a writer. He is passionate about football, and is also a singer-songwriter.

ABOUT THE ARTIST

Tony Ross is considered to be one of the finest children's illustrators in the country and his books are published all over the world. He has illustrated over eight hundred books for children, many of which have been rated modern classics. His books include *Tadpole's Promise*, *I Hate School*, and the Damian Drooth, Supersleuth series as well as the bestselling Little Princess books which have now been made into an award-winning animated TV series.

READ MORE ABOUT MS WIZ
in these other two-in-one
bind-ups of Ms Wiz stories:

TOTALLY SPACED, MS WIZ

Two stories about Class Five's favourite
teacher, the paranormal operative, Ms Wiz.
First she's taking a puppy back home, far far
across the galaxy, and all without a spacesuit!
And then she's taking the whole class to the
tropical island of Sombrero.
What a great field trip!

'Bursting with life and vitality' *Carousel*

ISBN 9781842707029 £4.99

FANGTASTIC, MS WIZ

Ms Wiz is the new teacher for Class Five –
and they think she's just magic, from her black
nail polish to her pet talking rat, Herbert!
Ms Wiz spells Trouble, all right! And in the
second story, Ms Wiz meets someone very
special at the Christmas dance. She thinks he's
Dracula – but who is he really?

'Fast-paced adventures with a lovely sense
of humour' *Ultimate First Book Guide*

ISBN 9781842707036 £4.99

MS WIZ ROCKS

Podge would love to be a great musician,
but all the neighbours are complaining and
even his teacher is giving up. So who would
have thought his street band would make it
on TV in a talent contest? Is it only because
Ms Wiz is also in the band? And Ms Wiz is
the only one who can help Lizzie find her cat
when the fur-nappers are busy. But was it
really necessary to turn Lizzie into a cat?

Praise for earlier Ms Wiz titles:
'Every time I pick up a Ms Wiz, I'm totally
spell-bound . . . a wonderfully funny and
exciting read.' *Books for Keeps*

ISBN 9781842708484 £4.99